Disney's
Fantasyland

Including Mother Goose, Mickey and the Beanstalk,
The Three Little Pigs

A GOLDEN BOOK • NEW YORK
Western Publishing Company, Inc., Racine, Wisconsin 53404

© 1989 The Walt Disney Company. Stories and illustrations in this book previously copyrighted © 1988, 1949, 1948 The Walt Disney Company. All rights reserved. Printed in the U.S.A. No part of this book may be reproduced or copied in any form without written permission from the copyright owner. GOLDEN, GOLDEN & DESIGN, A GOLDEN BOOK, and A GOLDEN TREASURY are trademarks of Western Publishing Company, Inc. Library of Congress Catalog Card Number: 89-84577 ISBN: 0-307-15753-9/ISBN: 0-307-65753-1 (lib. bdg.)   MCMXCII

Mother Goose

THE QUEEN OF HEARTS

The queen of hearts,
    She made some tarts,
All on a summer's day.
The knave of hearts,
    He stole those tarts,
And with them ran away.

The king of hearts
    Called for those tarts,
And beat the knave full sore;
The knave of hearts
    Brought back those tarts,
And said he'd steal no more.

HEY, DIDDLE, DIDDLE

Hey, diddle, diddle, the cat and the fiddle,
The cow jumped over the moon;
The little dog laughed to see such sport,
And the dish ran away with the spoon.

CROSS PATCH

Cross patch,
Draw the latch,
Sit by the fire and spin;
Take a cup
And drink it up,
And call your neighbors in.

LITTLE JACK HORNER

Little Jack Horner sat in a corner,
Eating a Christmas pie;
He put in his thumb, and took out a plum,
And said, "What a good boy am I!"

JACK SPRAT

Jack Sprat could eat no fat,
His wife could eat no lean;
And so betwixt them both, you see,
They licked the platter clean.

LITTLE BETTY BLUE

Little Betty Blue
    Lost her holiday shoe.
What shall little Betty do?
    Buy her another
To match the other,
    And then she'll walk in two.

JUMPING JOAN

Here am I, little Jumping Joan.
When nobody's with me,
I'm always alone.

DEEDLE, DEEDLE DUMPLING

Deedle, deedle dumpling, my son John,
Went to bed with his stockings on;
One shoe off and one shoe on,
Deedle, deedle dumpling, my son John.

THIS LITTLE PIG

This little pig went to market,
This little pig stayed at home,
This little pig had roast beef,
This little pig had none,
This little pig cried, "Wee-wee-wee!"
All the way home.

MARY'S LAMB

Mary had a little lamb,
Its fleece was white as snow;
And everywhere that Mary went
The lamb was sure to go.

It followed her to school one day,
Which was against the rule;
It made the children laugh and play
To see a lamb at school.

ONE TO TEN

1, 2, 3, 4, 5,
I caught a hare alive;
6, 7, 8, 9, 10,
I let him go again.

JACK, BE NIMBLE

Jack, be nimble,
    Jack, be quick,
Jack, jump over
    The candlestick.

PETER, PETER, PUMPKIN-EATER

Peter, Peter, pumpkin-eater,
Had a wife and couldn't keep her;
He put her in a pumpkin shell,
And there he kept her very well.

HANDY PANDY

Handy Pandy, Jack-a-dandy,
Loved plum cake and sugar candy;
He bought some at a grocer's shop,
And out he came, hop, hop, hop.

THIS IS THE WAY THE LADIES RIDE

This is the way the ladies ride:
Trot, trot!   Trot, trot!   Trot, trot!

This is the way the gentlemen ride:
Gallop-a-trot!   Gallop-a-trot!

This is the way the farmers ride:
Hobbledy-hoy!   Hobbledy-hoy!

SIMPLE SIMON

Simple Simon met a pieman,
  Going to the fair;
Says Simple Simon to the pieman,
  "Let me taste your ware."

Says the pieman to Simple Simon,
  "Show me first your penny."
Says Simple Simon to the pieman,
  "Indeed I have not any."

He went to catch a dickey-bird
  And thought he could not fail,
Because he'd got a little salt
  To put upon his tail.

Simple Simon went a-fishing,
  For to catch a whale;
All the water he had got
  Was in his mother's pail.

He went for water in a sieve,
  But soon it all ran through,
And now poor Simple Simon
  Bids you all adieu.

DING, DONG, BELL

Ding, dong, bell,
Pussy's in the well!
Who put her in?
Little Johnny Green.
Who pulled her out?
Big Johnny Stout.
What a naughty boy was that
To try to drown poor pussy cat,
Who never did him any harm,
But killed the mice in his father's barn.

A DILLAR, A DOLLAR

A dillar, a dollar,
A ten o'clock scholar,
What makes you come so soon?
You used to come at ten o'clock,
And now you come at noon.

BOBBY SHAFTOE

Bobby Shaftoe's gone to sea,
Silver buckles at his knee;
He'll come back and marry me—
Pretty Bobby Shaftoe!

THERE WERE
TWO BLACKBIRDS

There were two blackbirds,
    Sitting on a hill,
The one named Jack,
    The other named Jill.

Fly away, Jack!
    Fly away, Jill!
Come again, Jack!
    Come again, Jill!

OLD KING COLE

Old King Cole was a merry old soul,
And a merry old soul was he;
He called for his pipes and he called for his bowl,
And he called for his fiddlers three!

HUMPTY DUMPTY

Humpty Dumpty sat on a wall,
Humpty Dumpty had a great fall;
All the king's horses and all the king's men
Couldn't put Humpty Dumpty together again.

THE OLD WOMAN WHO LIVED IN A SHOE

There was an old woman who lived in a shoe;
She had so many children she didn't know what to do.
She gave them some broth, without any bread;
She whipped them all soundly and sent them to bed.

ROCK-A-BYE, BABY

Rock-a-bye, baby,
On the treetop!
When the wind blows,
The cradle will rock;
When the bough breaks,
The cradle will fall;
Down will come baby,
Cradle and all.

RUB-A-DUB-DUB

Rub-a-dub-dub,
Three men in a tub,
And who do you think they be?
The butcher, the baker,
The candlestick maker.
Turn 'em out, knaves all three.

JACK AND JILL

Jack and Jill went up the hill
 To fetch a pail of water.
Jack fell down and broke his crown,
 And Jill came tumbling after.

Up Jack got, and home did trot,
 As fast as he could caper;
Went to bed and plastered his head
 With vinegar and brown paper.

LITTLE MISS MUFFET

Little Miss Muffet
Sat on a tuffet,
Eating her curds and whey.
Along came a spider
Who sat down beside her
And frightened Miss Muffet away!

HICKORY, DICKORY, DOCK

Hickory, dickory, dock,
The mouse ran up the clock.
The clock struck one,
The mouse ran down;
Hickory, dickory, dock.

LITTLE TOMMY TUCKER

Little Tommy Tucker
    Sings for his supper.
What shall he eat?
    White bread and butter.

How shall he cut it
    Without e'er a knife?
How shall he marry
    Without any wife?

GEORGIE PORGIE

Georgie Porgie, pudding and pie,
Kissed the girls and made them cry.
When the boys came out to play,
Georgie Porgie ran away.

Mickey and the Beanstalk

Far, far away, where the trees were greener than the prettiest green and the sky was bluer than the brightest blue, there was a place called Happy Valley. In Happy Valley the brooks babbled, the birds sang, and everyone smiled all day long.

High on a hill, overlooking Happy Valley, stood a magnificent castle. In the castle was the Golden Harp, who sang all day and cast a magic spell of happiness over the land.

But one day a terrible thing happened in Happy
Valley. Someone stole the Golden Harp from the castle,
and the magic spell of happiness was gone.

The birds stopped singing. The brooks stopped babbling. The crops stopped growing. The cows stopped giving milk. And all the people of Happy Valley grew sad and hungry.

"We must do something," said Farmer Donald.
"We'll starve if we don't," added Farmer Goofy.
"I know!" said Farmer Mickey. "I'll sell Bossy the cow and buy some food."

Mickey took the cow into town and sold her. When he returned, he said, "I have sold Bossy for three wonderful beans."

"Three beans!" cried Donald and Goofy. "We can't live on three beans!" Donald threw the beans on the floor in disgust.

"But...but...they are magic beans," said Mickey as he sadly watched the beans roll through a crack in the floor.

But Goofy and Donald didn't pay any attention to what Mickey was saying. They were too tired and hungry to listen.

During the night a moonbeam shone through the
window and through the crack in the floor onto the
beans.

The beans sprouted and began to grow. They grew
into a stalk that lifted the house. The beanstalk climbed
all the way up to the sky.

In the morning the hungry farmers woke up and looked out the window.

To their surprise Happy Valley was gone! All they could see from their window was a tremendous castle.

"Let's go!" said Mickey. "Whoever lives in that big castle must have plenty of food to share!"

Mickey, Donald, and Goofy climbed up to the top
of the castle stairs and crawled under the front door.
On an enormous table they saw huge platters of food.
Mammoth pitchers of fresh cold milk waited for them.
The farmers quickly climbed up a table leg and ate,
drank, and laughed merrily.

As they were finishing their meal a tiny voice called
out to them.

"Who's that?" asked Mickey.

"It came from in there," said Donald, pointing to a
box that was on the table.

Mickey, Donald, and Goofy moved closer to the box. "Who are you?" they asked.

"It is I, the Golden Harp," said a soft voice. "A giant kidnapped me and brought me here to his castle to sing for him."

The farmers were very frightened to hear that the castle belonged to a giant. They were so frightened that they almost ran away.

"Wait!" cried Mickey suddenly. "We can't leave without the Golden Harp."

"You're right," said Goofy bravely. "We have to rescue her and save Happy Valley!"

Just then they heard loud footsteps. Everything in the room was shaking as the footsteps came closer and closer.

"You must hide!" cried the Golden Harp.

Mickey, Donald, and Goofy ran as quickly as they could to hide from the evil giant.

The giant stomped over to the table and picked up a giant sandwich in his giant hand. He was just about to take a bite when he noticed that the sandwich was moving.

"There's a mouse in my sandwich!" roared the giant.

"Oh, I'm sorry," said Mickey. "I had no idea this was your sandwich." He jumped from the sandwich to the giant's shirt and then slid down the giant's leg.

"Run!" shouted Mickey to Donald and Goofy.
The giant was furious. He chased the three farmers
around the room until they were cornered. The giant
reached down to scoop them up in his hand—but he
missed Mickey!

The great big giant put the tiny little farmers into the box with the Golden Harp. He locked the box and slipped the key into his great big pocket. Then he sat down in a chair to take a nap.

Mickey waited in his hiding place behind the pitcher. When the giant finally fell asleep, Mickey tiptoed over to the box and knocked.

"The key," whispered the Golden Harp. "Get the key out of his pocket."

Mickey hurried over to the sleeping giant. Very slowly and carefully he pulled the key out of the giant's pocket.

The giant mumbled something and stirred, but he did not wake up.

Mickey tiptoed back to the box and unlocked it.
Goofy and Donald climbed out and then quickly lifted
out the Golden Harp. The four were very quiet as they
made their way to the front door.

Just as they were sneaking past the giant, he opened
one eye and let out a giant roar.

Goofy and Donald ran with the Golden Harp in
their arms. Mickey realized the giant would catch them
unless he could do something to distract him.

"You can't catch me!" Mickey taunted. The angry
giant ran toward Mickey, who dived under a rug. "Over
here!" Mickey said, but the giant was not fast enough to
catch Mickey.

Mickey ran toward an open window. "So long!" he
shouted as he jumped outside.

Mickey ran to the beanstalk with the giant following close behind. He jumped onto the beanstalk and slid down in a flash.

Donald and Goofy grabbed a saw and cut down the beanstalk in the nick of time. The giant fell and crashed through the ground, all the way to the center of the earth.

The farmers took the Golden Harp back to her castle to sing, and from that time on, Happy Valley was happy once again. And happiest of all were the three brave farmers—Mickey, Donald, and Goofy!

The Three Little Pigs

Once upon a time there were three little pigs who
went out into the big world to build their homes and
seek their fortunes.

The first little pig did not like to work at all. He
quickly built himself a house of straw.

Then off he danced down the road, to see how his
brothers were getting along.

The second little pig was building himself a house, too. He did not like to work any better than his brother, so he had decided to build a quick and easy house of sticks.

Soon it was finished, too. It was not a very strong little house, but at least the work was done. Now the second little pig was free to do what he liked.

What he liked to do was to play his fiddle and dance. So while the first little pig tooted his flute, the second little pig sawed away on his fiddle, dancing as he played.

And as he danced he sang:

"*I built my house of sticks,*
I built my house of twigs.
With a hey diddle-diddle
I play on my fiddle,
And dance all kinds of jigs."

Then off danced the two little pigs down the road
together to see how their brother was getting along.

The third little pig was a sober little pig. He was building a house, too, but he was building his of bricks. He did not mind hard work, and he wanted a stout little, strong little house, for he knew that in the woods nearby there lived a big bad wolf who liked nothing better than to catch little pigs and eat them up!

So slap, slosh, slap! Away he worked, laying bricks and smoothing mortar between them.

"Ha, ha, ha!" laughed the first little pig, when he saw his brother hard at work.

"Ho, ho, ho!" laughed the second little pig. "Come down and play with us!" he called.

But the busy little pig did not pause. Slap, slosh, slap! went bricks on mortar as he called down to them:

"I build my house of stones.
I build my house of bricks.
I have no chance
To sing and dance,
For work and play don't mix."

"Ho, ho, ho! Ha, ha, ha!" laughed the two lazy little pigs, dancing along to the tune of the fiddle and the flute.

"You can laugh and dance and sing," their busy brother called after them, "but I'll be safe and you'll be sorry when the wolf comes to the door!"

"Ha, ha, ha! Ho, ho, ho!" laughed the two little pigs
again, and they disappeared into the woods, singing a
merry tune:

"Who's afraid of the big bad wolf,
The big bad wolf, the big bad wolf?
Who's afraid of the big bad wolf?
Tra la la la la-a-a-a!"

Just as the first pig reached his door, out of the woods popped the big bad wolf!

The little pig squealed with fright and slammed the door.

"Little pig, little pig, let me come in!" cried the wolf.

"Not by the hair of my chinny-chin-chin!" said the little pig.

"Then I'll huff, and I'll puff, and I'll blow your house in!" roared the wolf.

And he did. He blew the little straw house all to pieces!

Away raced the little pig to his brother's house of sticks. No sooner was he in the door than—knock, knock, knock—there was the big bad wolf!

But, of course, the little pigs would not let him come in.

"I'll fool those little pigs," said the big bad wolf to himself. He left the little pig's house, and he hid behind a big tree.

Soon the door opened and the two little pigs peeked out. There was no wolf in sight.

"Ha, ha, ha! Ho, ho, ho!" laughed the two little pigs.
"We fooled him."

Then they danced around the room, singing gaily:

"Who's afraid of the big bad wolf,
The big bad wolf, the big bad wolf?
Who's afraid of the big bad wolf?
Tra la la la la-a-a-a!"

Soon there came another knock at the door. It was the big bad wolf again, but he had covered himself with a sheepskin and was curled up in a big basket, looking like a little lamb.

"Who's there?" called the second little pig.

"I'm a poor little sheep, with no place to sleep. Please open the door and let me in," said the big bad wolf in a sweet little voice.

The little pig peeked through a crack in the door, and he could see the wolf's big black paws and sharp fangs.

"Not by the hair of my chinny-chin-chin!

"You can't fool us with that sheepskin!" said the second little pig.

"Then I'll huff, and I'll puff, and I'll blow your house in!" cried the angry old wolf.

So he *huffed*,
and he PUFFED,
and he *puffed*,
and he HUFFED,
and he blew the little twig house all to pieces!

Away raced the two little pigs, straight to the third little pig's house of bricks.

"Don't worry," said the third little pig to his two frightened little brothers. "You are safe here." Soon they were all singing gaily.

This made the big bad wolf perfectly furious!

"Now by the hair of my chinny-chin-chin!" he roared, "I'll huff, and I'll puff, and I'll blow your house in!"

So the big bad wolf *huffed*, and he PUFFED, and he *puffed*, and he HUFFED, but he could not blow down that little house of bricks! How could he get in? At last he thought of the chimney!

So up he climbed, quietly. Then, with a snarl, down he jumped—right into a kettle of boiling water!

With a yelp of pain he sprang straight back up the chimney and raced away into the woods. The three little pigs never saw him again, and they spent their time in the strong little brick house, singing and dancing merrily.